M N O P I could go on — all day Q R

S T al - pha - bet - i - cally speak-ing you're o - kay — U made my life com -plete

V means you're ver - y sweet W———— X Y Z — It's

fun to wan-der through the al-pha-bet with you to tell you what you mean to me! —

Dedicated to the children of the world—they are all beautiful.
S.L., B.K., and F.W.

For Caroline A.F.
M.A.

Text copyright © 1994 by Aria Music Co. and Budd Music Corp.
Illustrations copyright © 1994 by Martha Alexander

Based on the song "'A'—You're Adorable," words and music by
Buddy Kaye, Fred Wise, and Sidney Lippman; copyright © 1948,
renewed 1976 by Aria Music Co. and Budd Music Corp. (ASCSAP)

First edition 1994

Library of Congress Cataloging-in-Publication Data

Lippman, Sidney.
A you're adorable / words and music by Sidney Lippman, Buddy Kaye,
and Fred Wise ; illustrated by Martha Alexander.—1st ed.

Summary: An assortment of children and pets climb over, under, and
through the letters of the alphabet in this illustrated presentation of
a familiar song. Includes music.
ISBN 1-56402-237-4
1. Children's songs—Texts. [1. Alphabet. 2. Songs.] I. Kaye, Buddy.
II. Wise, Fred. III. Alexander, Martha G., ill. IV. Title.
PZ8.3.L635Yo   1994
[E]—dc20   93-931

10 9 8 7 6 5 4 3 2 1

Printed in Italy

The pictures in this book were
done in watercolor.

Candlewick Press
2067 Massachusetts Avenue
Cambridge, Massachusetts 02140

A You're Adorable

Words and music by Buddy Kaye, Fred Wise, and Sidney Lippman

Illustrated by
Martha Alexander

CANDLEWICK PRESS
CAMBRIDGE, MASSACHUSETTS

you're adorable

you're so beautiful

you're a cutie
full of charms

you're a
darling and

you're
exciting
and

you're a
feather
in my arms

you look good to me

you're so heavenly

you're the
one I idolize

we're like
Jack and Jill

you're

so

kissable

is the
lovelight
in your eyes

I could go on all day

alphabetically speaking, you're okay

made my
life complete

means you're
very sweet

It's fun to wander through

the alphabet with you

to tell you
what you mean
to me!

I   L-O-V-E   Y-O-U,

I   <u>R</u>   <u>N</u>   ♡

with   you!

A you're a-dor-a-ble B you're so beau-ti-ful C you're a cu-tie full of charms

D you're a dar-ling and E you're ex-cit-ing and F you're a feath-er in my arms

G you look good to me H you're so hea-ven-ly I you're the one I i-dol-ize

J we're like Jack and Jill K you're so kiss-a-ble L is the love-light in your eyes